the king's singers

SPIRITUALS

THE COLOUR OF SONG
VOLUME 3

I0901432

ISBN 978-0-634-06190-5

the colour of song

EXCLUSIVELY DISTRIBUTED BY
HAL•LEONARD® CORPORATION
7777 W. BLUEMOUND RD. P.O. BOX 13819 MILWAUKEE, WI 53213

SPIRITUALS
The Colour of Song (Vol. 3)

At a performance by the King's Singers, audiences throughout the world experience a wide range of emotions depicted in the group's vast repertoire – joy, sadness, love, anger, jealousy, laughter. The range of vocal colours used is no less wide, and by the end of the concert the audiences perhaps realize that the human voice is capable of much more than simply speaking or singing. The King's Singers call this total experience "The Colour of Song." This series of songbooks aims to reflect the variety of repertoire and performing technique which is found in each of the musical periods and styles the King's Singers explore in their concert work – from Byrd to the Beatles! We hope these collections will enrich your concert repertoire.

Arrangements of spirituals have formed part of the King's Singers' repertoire from the very early days, with books like *Songs of Yale* providing a good source of material before the group had discovered its own arrangers. Now, as with all sections of the King's Singers library, the genre is very amply represented. We draw from it particularly when we need music to round off a concert in a European church or cathedral, where some light relief is needed after the seriousness of Byrd, Gesualdo or whoever. Here, we select some of the current favourites, including two, "Deep River" and "Down to the River to Pray," which were arranged especially for this volume.

Arrangement/Performance Notes

Deep River *(arr. Philip Lawson)*
I arranged this classic spiritual for the many concerts we do in European cathedrals and churches, where the acoustics frequently help the warm textures to come through. In a concert hall situation this effect can be partially created by introducing a little breath into the sound in the soft passages, which makes a nice contrast with the more "voiced" sound which can be employed in the loud passages. That being said, the loud singing should always be sonorous and never edgy. There are two completely different versions of the verse, and as I couldn't decide which to use, I incorporated both.

Down to the River to Pray *(arr. Philip Lawson)*
It was the film *O Brother, Where Art Thou?* which drew our attention to this fine traditional song. Try a hard, folky tone for the solos and duets, and contrast with a warm, breathy texture for the six-part verse.

Joshua *(arr. Robert Sells)*
This arrangement dates back to the time when the original King's Singers were at Cambridge, but it is still a winner today. Sing the running quaver passages smoothly and they won't feel or sound too difficult. You can raise the roof with the fortissimo finish!

Keep in the Middle of the Road *(arr. David Overton)*
The humorous elements of this arrangement should be brought out (the banjo passage, big dynamic contrasts, the very fast ending, etc.). You must always be aware of where the melody is and take care not to obscure it with accompaniment.

Rise Up, Shepherd, and Follow *(arr. Carl Davis)*
This arrangement calls for legato singing, but with lots of energy, especially in the soft passages which must always "travel." Although the "up" of "rise up" sometimes has a staccato mark, it should never be too clipped. We altered Carl's dynamic scheme slightly, but feel we've found a shape which works for us. You can of course change any dynamics which don't suit your group in this and any of our arrangements.

Sometimes I Feel Like a Motherless Child *(arr. Carl Davis)*
This simple setting was arranged for Marilyn Horne, and although we have to rework it slightly for six voices, we here present it in its original form. If you are performing it with a small group, the solo, while obviously quite dramatic, should not be allowed to dominate the texture too much, as the chords of the accompanying voices are integral to the success of the piece.

Stand Still, Jordan *(arr. A.P. Jackman)*
This was arranged for us in 1994 and is one of Andrew Jackman's more virtuosic efforts. It requires great energy and attention to detail. In places where the chords flash past very quikly, each chord has to be voiced so that unimportant notes are subdued. In other words, the vocal lines at these points must not be sung as solo lines, but rather "maneuvered" to make each chord work.

Standing in the Need of Prayer *(arr. Simon Park)*
This is an almost light-hearted arrangement in spite of the text. It needs a very united sound throughout and don't let the quavers run away with themselves. Use the extremes of dynamics marked later in the piece to full effect.

Swing Low, Sweet Chariot *(arr. Peter Knight)*
An old favorite of ours. Peter Knight's feel for choral texture is seen here at its finest. The block passages need a firm bass line to make the chords ring.

Philip Lawson

Deep River

For SATTBB a cappella
Performance Time: Approx. 4:00

Traditional Spiritual
Arranged by PHILIP LAWSON

13
mf
Oh, don't you want to go to that gos - pel feast,
Unis.
camp - ground. Oo gos - pel feast, that prom - ised land where
mf
camp - ground. Oo prom - ised land where
mf
camp - ground. Oo prom - ised land where
Unis. mf
camp - ground. Oo prom - ised land where
13
mf
12
dim.
mp
all is peace? Lord, Deep riv - er deep, deep riv - er deep,
dim.
mp
all is peace? Lord, Deep riv - er deep, deep riv - er deep,
dim.
mp
all is peace? Lord, I want to cross o - ver in - to camp - ground.
dim.
mp
all is peace? Lord, Deep, deep riv - er deep, deep riv - er
dim.
mp
16

21
Soprano
Alto
o - ver
Deep riv - er, my home is o - ver Jor - dan. Deep
Tenor I
Tenor I only
add Tenor II
Unis. mp
Tenor II
Deep riv - er, my home is o - ver Jor - dan. Deep
Baritone
Unis. mp
Bass
Deep
21
21
Unis.
riv - er, Lord, I want to cross o - ver in - to camp - ground. Oo
29 More movement
mf
riv - er, Oo camp - ground. Oo
Unis. mf
riv - er, Oo camp - ground. I'll go in - to heav - en and
29 More movement
26

rall. e dim.
Unis.
Oo I'll cast my crown at Je - sus' feet.
Oo I'll cast my crown at Je - sus' feet.
take my seat. I'll cast my crown at Je - sus' feet.
31
37 Tempo I
Soprano
Alto
Oo
Tenor I
Oo
Tenor II
Deep riv - er, my home is o - ver Jor - dan.
Baritone
Bass
Oo
37 Tempo I
R.H.
L.H.
37

Ah
camp - ground. Oh,
Ah
camp - ground. Oh,
Deep
riv - er, Lord, I want to cross o - ver in - to camp - ground. Oh,
Ah
camp - ground.
R.H.
L.H.
41
45
Soprano
Alto
Deep
riv - er, my home is o - ver Jor - dan. Deep
Tenor I
Jor - dan.
Tenor II
Deep
riv - er, my home is o - ver Jor - dan. Deep
Baritone
Bass
Deep
riv - er, my home is o - ver Jor - dan. Deep
45
45

53
Unis.
riv - er, Lord, I want to cross o - ver in - to camp-ground. Oh, when I get to heav - en I'll
riv - er, Lord, I want to cross o - ver in - to camp-ground. Oh, when I get to heav - en I'll
Unis.
riv - er, Lord, I want to cross o - ver in - to camp-ground. Oh, when I get to heav - en I'll
53
50
Lord, I want to cross o - ver in - to
Unis.
walk all a - bout. There's no one there to turn me out. Lord, Deep riv - er
walk all a - bout. There's no one there to turn me out. Lord, Deep riv - er
walk all a - bout. There's no one there to turn me out. Lord, Deep,
54

camp-ground. Deep riv - er deep,
61
dim.
deep, I want to cross o - ver in - to camp - ground. Deep riv - er
deep, Lord, I want to cross o - ver in - to
dim.
deep, deep riv - er deep, deep riv - er
dim.
deep riv - er deep, deep riv - er deep,
61
dim.
58
65
rit.
Unis.
a tempo
pp
deep, deep riv - er deep, Deep riv - er, my
camp - ground. Deep riv - er deep,
deep, I want to cross o - ver in - to camp - ground. Deep riv - er, my
deep riv - er deep, Deep riv - er, my
65
62

p
Unis.
home is o - ver Jor - dan. Deep riv - er, Lord, I want to cross o - ver in - to
p
home is o - ver Jor - dan. Deep riv - er, Oo
p
home is o - ver Jor - dan. Deep riv - er, Oo
p
67
73
pp
rit.
camp - ground. Deep riv - er deep, deep riv - er deep.
Deep riv - er deep, deep riv - er deep.
pp
rit.
pp
camp - ground. riv - er deep.
rit.
pp
camp - ground. riv - er deep.
73
pp
rit.
R.H.
72

Down to the River to Pray

For SATTBB a cappella
Performance Time: Approx. 2:35

Traditional
Arranged by PHILIP LAWSON

Tenor II
mp
35
As I went down in the riv - er to pray, stud - y - in' a -
Stagger breathing
Baritone
Bass
Mm (or Oo)
Piano (For rehearsal only)
35
33
bout that good old way and who shall wear the robe and
39
50
Soprano
mp Stagger breathing
Alto
Oo
Tenor II
crown. Good Lord, show me the way. Oh, broth - ers,
Baritone
Bass
(Oo)
50
45

* Optional Alto

good old way and who shall wear the star - ry crown. Good Lord,
good old way and who shall wear the star - ry crown. Good Lord,
73
83
show me the way Oh, fa - thers, let's go down,
show me the way Oh, fa - thers, let's go down,
83
80
let's go down, come on down. Oh, fa - thers, let's go
let's go down, come on down. Oh, fa - thers, let's go
87

Unis.
down, down in the riv - er to pray. As I went
down, down in the riv - er to pray.
94
101
Soprano
Alto
down in the riv - er to pray, stud - y - in' a - bout that good old way and
Tenor I
Tenor II
down in the riv - er to pray, stud - y - in' a - bout that good old way and
Baritone
Bass
down in the riv - er to pray, stud - y - in' a - bout that good old way and
101
who shall wear the robe and crown. Good Lord, show me the way.
who shall wear the robe and crown. Good Lord, show me the way.
who shall wear the robe and crown. Good Lord, show me the way.
108

116
cresc.
Oh, moth - ers, let's go down, come on down, don't you wan - na go down?
Oh, moth - ers, let's go down, come on down, don't you wan - na go down?
Oh, moth - ers, let's go down, come on down, don't you wan - na go down?
116

mp
Come on, moth - ers, let's go down, down in the riv - er to pray.
Come on, moth - ers, let's go down, down in the riv - er to pray.
Come on, moth - ers, let's go down, down in the riv - er to pray.
124

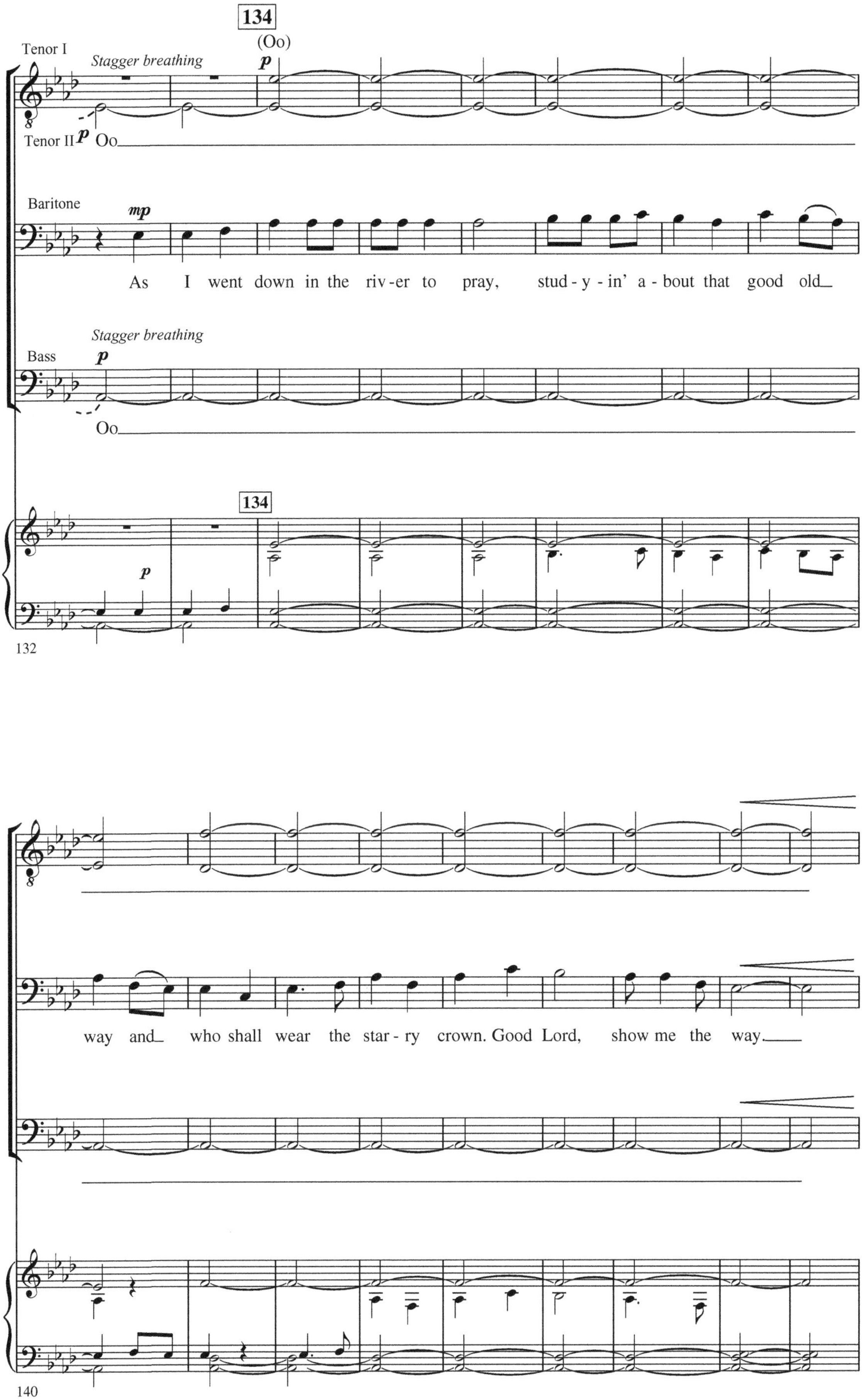
134
(Oo)
Tenor I
Stagger breathing
p
Tenor II p Oo
Baritone
mp
As I went down in the riv-er to pray, stud-y-in' a-bout that good old
Stagger breathing
Bass p
Oo
132
way and who shall wear the star-ry crown. Good Lord, show me the way.
140

149
Soprano
mf
Alto
Oh, down, down, down.
Tenor I
mf
Tenor II
Oh, down, down, down.
Baritone
mf
Oh, sin - ners, let's go down, let's go down, come on down
Bass
mf
Oh, down, down, down.
149
mf
149

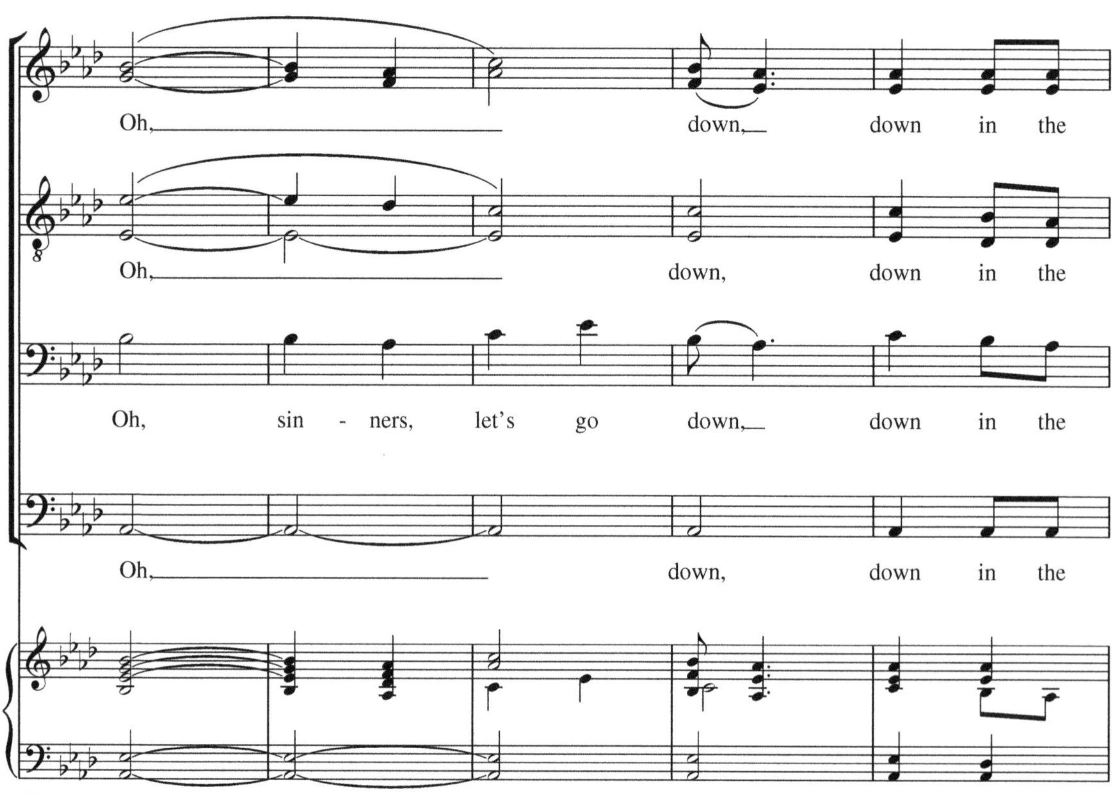
Oh, down, down in the
Oh, down, down in the
Oh, sin - ners, let's go down, down in the
Oh, down, down in the
157

dim.
p As I went
riv - er to pray.
riv - er to pray.
riv - er to pray.
riv - er to pray.
p
162
169 (Sop. only)
169 down in the riv - er to pray, stud - y - in' a - bout that
174 good old way and who shall wear the robe and
rit.
179 crown. Good Lord, show me the way.

Joshua

For TTBB a cappella
Performance Time: Approx. 1:50

Traditional Spiritual
Arranged by ROBERT SELLS

Jer - i - cho, Jer - i - cho, Jer - i - cho.
Jer - i - cho, Jer - i - cho, Jer - i - cho.
bat - tle of Jer - i - cho, Jer - i - cho.
Yeh! Yeh! Yeh! Oh,
6
Josh - ua fit the bat - tle of Jer - i - cho, and the walls come tum - blin'
Josh - ua fit the bat - tle of Jer - i - cho, and the walls come tum - blin'
Josh fit the bat - tle, and the walls come tum - blin'
Yeh! Yeh! and the walls come tum - blin'
9

12 Allegro vivace (♩ = ca. 168)
down.
down. Josh - ua fit the bat - tle
down. Josh - ua fit the bat - tle
Oh, Yeh! Oh, Yeh! Oh, Yeh! Josh - ua fit the bat - tle
12 Allegro vivace (♩ = ca. 168)
12
div.
(Hum) (open to Ah)
of Jer - i - cho. Josh - ua fit the bat - tle of Jer - i - cho.
of Jer - i - cho. Josh - ua fit the bat - tle of Jer - i - cho.
of Jer - i - cho. Oh, Yeh! Josh - ua fit the bat - tle of Jer - i - cho. Oh,
15

18
Josh - ua fit the bat - tle of Jer - i - cho, Jer - i - cho,
Josh - ua fit the bat - tle of Jer - i - cho, Jer - i - cho,
Josh fit the bat - tle of Jer - i - cho,
Yeh! Yeh! Yeh!
18
18
Jer - i - cho. Josh - ua fit the bat - tle of Jer - i - cho, and the
Jer - i - cho. Josh - ua fit the bat - tle of Jer - i - cho, and the
Jer - i - cho. Josh fit the bat - tle, and the
Yeh! Oh, Yeh! Yeh! and the
21

walls come tum - blin' down.
walls come tum - blin' down.
Up
walls come tum - blin' down.
Up
walls come tum - blin' down.
walls come tum - blin', Oh, Yeh! Oh, Yeh! Oh,
24

27
to the walls of Jer - i - cho, he marched with spear in
to the walls of Jer - i - cho, he marched with spear in
Jer - i - cho, he marched with spear in
Yeh! Up to the walls of Jer - i - cho, he marched with spear in
27
27

hand. Blow_ them_ ram - horns,__ Josh - u - a cried, 'cause_ the
hand.___ Blow_ them_ ram - horns,__ Josh - u - a cried, 'cause_ the
hand. Blow_ them ram-horns, Josh - u - a cried, 'cause_ the
hand.___ Blow_ them_ ram - horns,__ Josh - u - a cried, 'cause_ the
30
35
bat - tle is in my hand.___ Then the lam',_ ram,_ sheep - horns be -
bat - tle is__ in__ my hand.___ Then the lam',_ ram, sheep-horns be -
bat - tle is in__ my hand.___
bat - tle is__ in__ my_ hand.___ Lam', ram, the
33

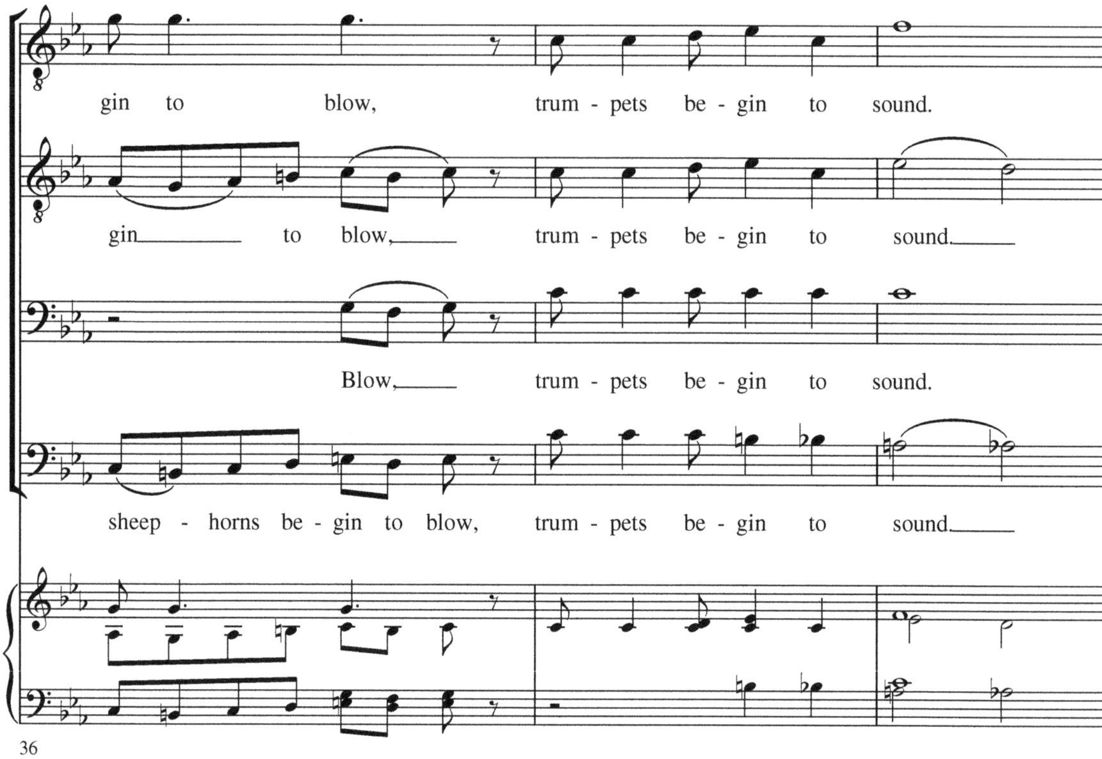
gin to blow, trum - pets be - gin to sound.
gin to blow, trum - pets be - gin to sound.
Blow, trum - pets be - gin to sound.
sheep - horns be - gin to blow, trum - pets be - gin to sound.
36

Josh - u - a com-mand - ed the chil-dren to shout, and the walls come tum - blin'
Josh - u - a com-mand - ed the chil-dren to shout, and the walls come tum - blin'
Josh - u - a com-mand - ed the chil-dren to shout, and the walls come tum - blin'
Josh - u - a com-mand - ed the chil-dren to shout, and the walls come tum - blin'
39

molto rit.
43 Slow, accel. poco a poco al fine
down.
p cresc. poco a poco al fine
Josh-ua fit the bat-tle of Jer - i - cho.
down, Oh, Yeh! Josh-ua fit the bat-tle of Jer - i - cho. Oh,
42
cresc. poco a poco al fine
(Hum)
div.
47
Josh - ua fit the bat - tle of
Josh fit the
Yeh! Josh-ua fit the bat-tle of Jer - i - cho. Oh, Yeh!
45

Jer - i - cho, Jer - i - cho, Jer - i - cho.
Jer - i - cho, Jer - i - cho, Jer - i - cho.
bat - tle of Jer - i - cho, Jer - i - cho.
Yeh! Yeh! Yeh! Oh,
48
down.
(Opt.)
ff allarg.
Josh-ua fit the bat-tle of Jer - i - cho, and the walls come tum - blin' down.
ff allarg.
Josh-ua fit the bat-tle of Jer - i- cho, and the walls come tum - blin' down.
ff allarg.
Josh fit the bat - tle, and the walls come tum - blin' down.
ff allarg.
div.
Yeh! Yeh! come tum - blin' down.
ff allarg.
51

Keep in the Middle of the Road

For SATBBB a cappella
Performance Time: Approx. 2:25

Traditional Spiritual
Arranged by DAVID OVERTON

Soprano
Unis.
Alto
Right in the mid-dle of the road.
In the mid-dle,
in the mid-dle,
in the
Tenor
Then chil-dren keep in the mid-dle,
in the mid-dle,
in the
Bar. I
Unis.
Bar. II
Then chil-dren keep in the mid-dle of the road.
Chil - dren keep in the
Bass
Of the road,
in the mid-dle,
in the mid-dle,
in the
17
15
mid - dle, Don't you look to the right, don't you look to the left, but keep in the mid-dle of the
mid - dle, Don't you look, don't you look, but keep in the mid-dle of the
mid - dle of the road. Don't you look to the right, don't you look to the left, but keep in the mid-dle of the
mid - dle, Don't you look to the right, don't you look to the left, but keep in the mid-dle of the
20

Sop.
Alto
Tenor
Bar. I
Bar. II
Bass
25
road.
road.
road. I ain't got time for to stop and talk, Keep in the mid-dle of the road. 'Cause the
road. I ain't got time for to stop and talk,
road, in the mid-dle of the road.
24
33
I'll fix my eyes on the
road is rough and it's hard to walk, Keep in the mid-dle of the road. Fix my eyes on the
Keep in the mid-dle of the road. 'Cause the road is rough and it's hard to walk, Fix my eyes on the
I'll fix my eyes on the
29

Tenor
stronger
gold-en stair, And I'll keep on a-go-ing till I get there.'Cause my head is bound for the crown to wear.
Bar. I
Unis.
stronger
Unis.
Bar. II
gold-en stair, And I'll keep on a-go-ing till I get there.'Cause my head is bound for the crown to wear.
Bass
stronger
gold-en stair, And I'll keep on a-go-ing till I get there.'Cause my head is bound for the crown to wear.
34
Sop.
Unis.
41
Alto
Keep in the mid-dle of the road. Then chil-dren keep in the mid-dle of the road.
Tenor
Keep in the mid-dle of the road. Then chil - dren keep, mid-dle of the
Bar. I
Unis.
Bar. II
Keep in the mid-dle of the road. Then chil-dren,
Bass
Keep in the mid-dle of the road. Then chil - dren keep,
41
39

mf
Chil - dren keep, mid-dle of the road, of the road, but
Don't you look to the right, don't you look to the left, but
Unis.
Chil-dren keep in the mid-dle of the road. but
Chil - dren keep, mid-dle of the road, of the road,
43
Sop.
keep in the mid-dle of the road. Come and join the
Alto
keep in the mid-dle of the road. Come and
Tenor
keep in the mid-dle of the road. of the, Come and
Bar. I
Unis.
Bar. II keep in the mid-dle of the road. in the mid-dle of the road.
Bass
keep in the mid-dle of the road, in the mid - dle of the road, in the mid-dle of the road.
50
47

f
wea - ry band, 'Cause we're bound for home in the
mf
join our band, Bound for the
mf
join our band, Bound for the
pp
Keep in the mid-dle of the road.
pp
Keep in the mid-dle of the road.
pp
mf
51
58
ff
hap - py land. Turn your back on this world of sin.
ff
hap - py land. Turn your back on this world of sin.
ff
hap - py land. Just
pp
ff
Keep in the mid-dle of the road. Just
pp
Keep in the mid-dle of the road.
58
pp
ff
55

Sop.
Alto
Tenor
Bar. I
Bar. II
Bass
Unis.
ff
Knock at the door and they'll let you in. 'Cause you're nev - er gon - na get such a chance a - gain.
knock at the door and they'll let you in. 'Cause you're nev - er gon - na get such a chance a - gain.
knock at the door and they'll let you in. 'Cause you're nev - er gon - na get such a chance a - gain.
Knock at the door and they'll let you in. 'Cause you're nev - er gon - na get such a chance a - gain.
60
66
mf
mp
(Banjo effect)
Then chil - dren keep in the mid - dle of the road. Chil - dren keep in the
- dren - dren - dren Brr - dren - dren
- dren - dren - dren Brr - dren - dren
Keep in the mid-dle of the road. Then chil - chil - chil - Brr chil - chil -
64

Unis.
mid-dle of the road. Don't you look to the right, don't you look to the left, but keep in the mid-dle of the
-dren Brr chem chem chem chem chem chem Brr in,
Unis.
-dren Brr chem chem chem chem chem chem Brr in, of,
chil- Brr chem chem chem chem chem chem Brr Bom bom
69
Sop.
74 Slightly Faster
Then keep in mid of the
Alto
road. Then keep in mid of the
Tenor
This world is full of sin-ful things, Keep in the mid-dle of the
Bar. I
road. Keep in the mid-dle of the
Bar. II
road. Then keep in mid of the
Bass
bom bom bom bom bom Then keep in mid of the
74 Slightly Faster
73

road. Oh_yeah!
road. Oh yeah!
road.
Put_ on them wings.
road. When the feet get tired_ put on_ them wings. Keep in the mid-dle of the road.
road. Oh yeah!
Put_ on, put on them wings.
road. Oh yeah!
Put_ on, on them wings. If you
77
82
Slowly and freely
Sop.
rit.
Unis.
Alto
You can put on wings an'
Tenor
You can watch them an - gels in the sky.
Bar. I
Unis.
Bar. II
You can watch them in the sky. You can put on wings an'
Bass
lay down in the road and die
You can watch them in the sky.
82
Slowly and freely
rit.
82

Tempo I
Unis.
90
get up an' fly. Keep in the mid-dle of the road. Then keep in the
Keep in the mid-dle of the road. Then chil-dren keep in the
get up an' fly. Keep in the mid-dle of the road. Then chil-dren keep in the
Keep in the mid-dle of the road. Then chil-dren keep in the
87
mid-dle of the road. Keep in the mid-dle of the road. Don't you
mid-dle of the road. Chil-dren keep in the mid-dle of the road. Don't you
mid-dle of the road. Chil-dren keep in the mid-dle of the road. Don't you
mid-dle of the, mid-dle of the road. Keep in the mid-dle of the road. Don't you
91

96 Very fast
Sop.
Alto
Tenor
Bar. I
Bar. II
Bass
look to the right, don't you look to the left, but
keep in the middle of the road, in the middle of the
94
keep in the mid-dle
keep in the mid-dle of the, mid-dle of the road.
mid-dle of the road, in the mid-dle of the road.
road, in the mid-dle of the, mid-dle of the road.
road, in the mid-dle of the, mid-dle of the, keep in the mid-dle of the road.
Slow
cresc.
98

Rise Up, Shepherd, and Follow

For SATTBB a cappella
Performance Time: Approx. 2:15

Traditional Spiritual
Arranged by CARL DAVIS

9
p
mf
Fol - low, fol - low, Rise up, shep-herd, and fol - low, Fol-low the star of
Fol - low, fol - low, Rise up, shep-herd, and fol - low, Fol-low the star of
Fol - low, fol - low, Rise up, shep-herd, and fol - low, Fol-low the star of
Fol - low, fol - low, Rise up, shep-herd, and fol - low, Fol-low the star of
Fol - low, fol - low, Rise up, shep-herd, and fol - low, Fol-low the star of
Fol - low, fol - low, Rise up, shep-herd, and fol - low, Fol-low the star of
9
17
f
f with energy
Beth - le - hem, shep-herd, and fol - low.
Beth - le - hem, shep-herd, and fol - low.
Beth - le - hem, Rise up, shep-herd, and fol - low.
Beth - le - hem, Rise up, shep-herd, and fol - low. There's a star in the East on
Beth - le - hem, Rise up, shep-herd, and fol - low.
Beth - le - hem, Rise up, shep-herd, and fol - low.
14

Rise up, shep-herd, and fol - low,
Rise up, shep-herd, and fol - low,
Rise up, shep-herd, and fol - low,
Christ - mas morn,
It will lead to the place where the
Rise up, shep-herd, and fol - low,
Rise up, shep-herd, and fol - low,
18
Rise up, shep-herd, and fol - low. Leave your sheep and leave your lambs,
Rise up, shep-herd, and fol - low. Leave your sheep and leave your lambs,
Rise up, shep-herd, and fol - low. Leave your sheep and leave your lambs,
Sav - ior's born. Rise up, shep-herd, and fol - low. Leave your sheep and leave your lambs,
Rise up, shep-herd, and fol - low. Leave your sheep and leave your lambs,
Rise up, shep-herd, and fol - low. Leave your sheep and leave your lambs,
25
22

Rise up, shep-herd, and fol - low, Leave your ewes and leave your rams,
Rise up, shep-herd, and fol - low, Leave your ewes and leave your rams,
Rise up, shep-herd, and fol - low, Leave your ewes and leave your rams,
Rise up, shep-herd, and fol - low, Leave your ewes and leave your rams,
Rise up, shep-herd, and fol - low, Leave your ewes and leave your rams,
Rise up, shep-herd, and fol - low, Leave your ewes and leave your rams,
27
33
p
and fol - low.
fol - low.
Rise up, shep-herd, and fol-low.
f
Rise up, shep-herd, and fol - low If you take good heed of the an-gel's words,
Rise up, shep-herd, and fol - low
Rise up, shep-herd, and fol - low
31

mp legato
Rise up, shep-herd, and fol - low,
You'll for-get your flock, you'll for - get your herds.
f
mp
35

mf
Rise up, shep-herd, and fol - low.
41
p
Fol - low, fol - low,
Leave your sheep and leave your lambs,
39

f
Rise up, shep-herd, and fol - low, Leave your ewes and leave your rams,
dim.
Rise and follow, follow, follow.
Rise up, shep-herd, and fol - low, fol - low, fol - low.
43
47

51
mp cresc. poco a poco
Fol - low, fol - low, Rise up, shep-herd, and fol - low,
Follow the star of Beth-le-hem, Rise up, and fol - low.
Fol-low the star of Beth-le-hem, Rise up, shep-herd, and fol - low,
Fol-low the star of Beth-le-hem, Rise up, shep-herd, and fol - low, fol -
ff
55

60
mp
p
Fol - low, fol - low, Rise up, shep-herd, and
fol - low. Fol - low, fol - low, Rise up, shep-herd, and
fol - low. Fol - low, fol - low, Rise up, shep-herd, and
- low, fol - low. Rise up, shep-herd, and
- low, fol - low. Rise up, shep-herd, and
- low, fol - low. Rise up, shep-herd, and
59
fol - low, Fol-low the star of Beth - le - hem, and
fol - low, Fol-low the star of Beth - le - hem, Rise and
fol - low, Fol-low the star of Beth - le - hem, Rise up, shep-herd, and
fol - low, Fol-low the star of Beth - le - hem, Rise up, shep-herd, and
fol - low, Fol-low the star of Beth - le - hem, Rise up, shep-herd, and
fol - low, Fol-low the star of Beth - le - hem, Rise up, shep-herd, and
63

68
p
fol - low, fol - low, fol - low.
fol - low, fol - low, fol - low.
fol - low, fol - low,
fol - low, fol - low, fol - low,
fol - low, fol - low,
fol - low, fol - low, fol - low,
67
pp
fol - low, fol - low.
fol - low, fol - low.
fol - low, fol - low.
fol - low.
71

Sometimes I Feel Like a Motherless Child

For SATB div. and Solo a cappella
Performance Time: Approx. 3:00

Traditional Spiritual
Arranged by CARL DAVIS

some-times I feel like a moth-er-less child, a long way from home, a
some-times,
some-times, long way,
some-times, long way,
Ah long way,
9
15
f
mp
long way from home. True be-liev-er, a
long way from home. True be-liev-er,
long way from home. True be-liev-er,
long way from home. True be-liev-er,
long way from home. True be-liev-er,
13

long way from home, a long way from home.
p
long way home.
p
long way home.
p
long way, long way home.
p
long way home.
p
17
24
mp
Some-times I feel like I'm
p
Some - time, some - time,
p
Some - time, some - time,
p
Some - time, some - time,
24
21

al - most gone, some - times I feel like I'm al - most gone,
p
al - most gone,
some - time, al - most gone,
some - time, al - most gone,
25
some - times I feel like I'm al - most gone, way up in the
al - most gone, way
al - most gone, way
al - most gone, way
p
al - most gone, way
28

34
heav'n - ly land, way up in the heav'n - ly land.
up in the heav'n - ly land. True be -
up in the heav'n - ly land. True be -
up in the heav'n - ly land. True be -
up in the heav'n - ly land. True be -
34
31
True be - liev - er, way up in the heav'n - ly
sub. p
liev - er, true be - liev - er, up in the
liev - er, true be - liev - er, up in the
liev - er, true be - liev - er,
liev - er, true be - liev - er,
35

42
land, way up in the heav'n - ly land.
heav'n - ly land, way up in the heav'n - ly land.
heav'n - ly land, way up in the heav'n - ly land.
mp
Some-times I feel like a
mp
Some-times I feel like a
42
mp
39
mp
like a moth - er - less child,
mp
Some - times I feel like a moth - er - less child,
moth - er - less child, some - times I feel like a moth - er - less child,
moth - er - less child,
43

mp
Some-times I feel like a moth-er-less child, a long way from home, a
p
Ah long way from home,
p
Ah long way from home,
p
Ah long way from home,
p
Ah long way from home,
p
46
long way from home.
a long way, long way from home, way from home. Mm
a long way, long way from home, way from home. Mm
a long way, long way from home, way from home. Mm
a long way, long way from home, way from home. Mm
pp
50

Stand Still, Jordan

For SATTBB a cappella
Performance Time: Approx. 2:15

Traditional Spiritual
Arranged by A.P. JACKMAN

mf
No, no, no, no.
f
mf
f
mf
half spoken
Jor - dan, Lord, I can't stan' still. Hear me.
f
mf
f
mf
8
11
Unis. p
cresc. poco a poco
I got a moth-er in heav - en, I got a moth-er in heav - en,
p cresc. poco a poco
I got a moth-er in heav - en,
11
R.H.
cresc. poco a poco
11

Sop.
Alto
Ten. I
Ten. II
Bar.
Bass
Unis.
heav - en, Lord, I can't, no I can't stan'
I got a moth-er in heav - en, Lord, I can't stan'
15
19
still.
sub. quasi p (airy tone, animated)
mf cresc.
When I get up in glo - ry,
When I get up in
still, can't stan' still
sub. p
R.H.
cresc.
18

When I get up in glo - ry, Lord, I can't stan'
glo - ry, When I get up in glo - ry, Lord, I can't stan'
When I get up in glo - ry, Lord, I can't stan'
glo - ry, Bom (etc.)
22
can't stan' still, stan' still, can't stan' still
still, can't stan' still, stan' still, can't stan' still
still. Can't stan' still,
still. Can't stan' still,
Stan' still,
28
26

mp
Can't stan' still,
mp
Can't stan' still, Can't stan' still,
Can't stan' still, Can't stan' still, Can't stan' still,
Can't stan' still, Can't stan' still,
Jor - - dan, Stan' still, Jor - - dan,
29
p cresc.
Can't stan' still, Can't stan' still, Can't stan' still.
p cresc.
Can't stan' still, Can't stan' still, Can't stan' still.
mf
Can't stan' still.
f
ff
Stan' still, Jor - dan, Lord, I can't stan'
cresc.
32

f (marc.)
36
When that riv-er gon - na stan' still?
mp cresc.
Jor - dan
mp
When that riv-er gon - na stan' still? Jor - dan riv - er, Jor - dan
mp smooth
cresc.
still.
Doo doo (etc.)
35
dim.
Unis.
riv - er is chill-y an' cold.
pp cresc.
Oh, that Jor - dan riv - er is chill-y an', chill-y an' cold.
riv - er, riv-er,
riv - er, riv-er is chill-y an', chill-y an' cold.
riv-er,
39

44
pp
It will chill - a my bod - y,
Sop. only
bod -
no breath
p
cresc.
It will chill - a my bod - y, It will chill - a my bod - y,
It will chill - a my bod - y, It will chill - a my bod - y,
It will chill - a my bod - y, It will chill - a my bod - y,
It will chill - a my bod - y,
44
f
add Alto
marc.
mf
- - y, not my, not - a my soul.
It will chill - a my bod - y, but not my soul.
fp
chill my bod - y, not my, not - a my soul.
chill my bod - y,
chill my bod - y,
mf cresc.
48

52
f marc.
p f p f
marc.
ff
Stan' still, Jor - dan, Stan' still, Jor - dan, Stan' still,
Stan' still, Jor - dan, Stan' still, Jor - dan, Stan' still,
Stan' still, Jor - dan, Stan' still, Jor - dan, Stan' still,
Stan' still, Jor - dan, Stan' still, Jor - dan, Stan' still,
Stan' still, Jor - dan, Stan' still, Jor - dan, Stan' still,
Sop.
Lord, I can't stan' still. Ar - ee - oo -
Alto
Jor - dan, can't stan' still Ar - ee - oo -
Ten. I
Doot doot doot
Ten. II
Bar.
Doot doot doot
Bass
Hear me. Bom bom bom
60
sub. f
sub. p
57

62
fp
f driving
wah
Stan' still, Jor - dan,
fp
f driving
wah
Stan' still, Jor - dan,
sfz
mf
doot doot doot doot doot doot (etc.)
sfz
mf
doot doot doot doot doot doot (etc.)
sub. f
mf
bom bom bom bom bom bom bom bom bom (etc.)
62
sub. p
sub. f
mf
61
Stan' still, Jor - dan, Doot doot doot (etc.)
Stan' still, Jor - dan, Doot doot doot (etc.)
f
Oh, Doot doot Woh, Doot doot doot (etc.)
f Unis.
Woh, Stan' still, Jor - dan, Lord, I
f
f
64

Sop.
Alto
Unis.
70
No, no, no, no,
Ten. I
dim. poco a poco al fine
Lord, I can't stan'
Ten. II
Bar.
can't stan' still. No, no, no, no, Can't stan',
Bass
No, no, no, no, Can't stan',
68

dim. poco a poco al fine
no, no, no, no, Please help me, Lord.
still. Oh, I can't stan' still.
Unis.
no, no, no, no, Can't stan', Please help me, Lord.
no, no, no, no, Can't stan', Please help me, Lord. You know I
71

Can't stan',
Can't stan', Can't stan' still, Can't stan' still,
Can't stan' still, Can't stan' still,
can't stan', Can't stan' still, Can't stan' still,
74
p still.
p Doo
ten.
Can't stan' Doo doo doo
Doo doo doo
Can't stan' Doo doo
Can't stan' Doo doo doo
77

Standing in the Need of Prayer

For SATTBB a cappella
Performance Time: Approx. 2:10

Traditional Spiritual
Arranged by SIMON PARK

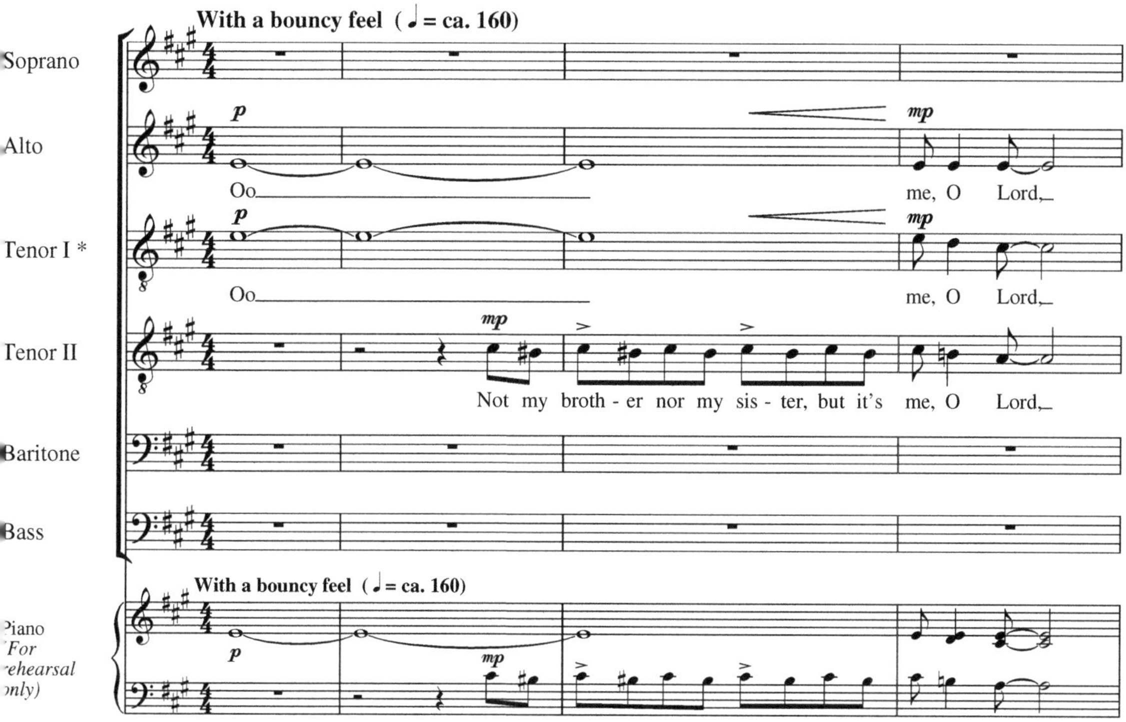

* Optional Alto

p
f
11
me, O Lord, stand-ing in the need of pray'r. It's me, it's
p
f
me, O Lord, stand-ing in the need of pray'r. It's me,
mp
p
f
me, O Lord, stand-ing in the need of pray'r. It's me,
mp
p
f
me, O Lord, stand-ing in the need of pray'r. It's me,
p
f
stand-ing in the need of pray'r. It's me, it's
p
f
stand-ing in the need of pray'r. It's me,
11
p
f
8

p
f
me, O Lord, stand-ing in the need of pray'r. It's me, it's
p
f
me, O Lord, stand-ing in the need of pray'r. It's me,
p
f
me, O Lord, stand-ing in the need of pray'r. It's me,
p
f
me, O Lord, stand-ing in the need of pray'r. It's me,
p
f
me, O Lord, stand-ing in the need of pray'r. It's me, it's
p
f
me, O Lord, stand-ing in the need of pray'r. It's me,
p
f
12

p
me, O Lord, stand-ing in the need of pray'r.
mf
Not the
16
19
mp
stand-ing in the need of
Oo
mf
me, O Lord,
preach - er but it's
nor the dea - con,

pray'r.
preach - er, dea - con, me, O Lord,
Not the preach - er nor the dea - con, but it's me, O Lord,
You know it's not the preach - er, dea - con, me, O Lord,
preach - er, dea - con, me, O Lord,
27
stand-ing in the need of pray'r. But it's me, it's me, O Lord,
stand-ing in the need of pray'r. But it's me, it's me, O Lord,
Oo It's not the preach-er, but it's me, it's me, O Lord,
Oo need of pray'r. But it's me, it's me, O Lord,
Oo need of pray'r. It's me, me, O Lord,
Oo need of pray'r. It's me, me, O Lord,

It's not the dea - con, but it's me,
stand - ing in the need of pray'r
But it's me,
stand - ing in the need of pray'r
It's me,
stand - ing in the need of pray'r
It's me,
stand - ing in the need of pray'r
It's me,
You know it's
29
me, O Lord,
stand - ing in the need of pray'r.
me, O Lord,
stand - ing in the need of pray'r.
me, O Lord,
stand - ing in the need of pray'r.
Not my fa - ther nor my moth - er, but it's
me, O Lord,
stand - ing in the need of pray'r
Oo
me, O Lord,
stand - ing in the need of pray'r
Oo
me, O Lord,
stand - ing in the need of pray'r
Oo
35 A little slower (♩ = ca. 120)
rall.
32

Oo standing in the need of pray'r.
Oo standing in the need of pray'r.
me, O Lord, It's not my
me, O Lord, standing in the need of pray'r.
standing in the need of pray'r.
36
rall.
Tempo I
O Lord, standing in the need of pray'r. It's
father, mother, me, O Lord, standing in the need of pray'r. It's
father nor my mother, but it's me, O Lord, standing in the need of pray'r. It's
father, mother, me, O Lord, standing in the need of pray'r.
father, mother, me, O Lord, standing in the need of pray'r.
father, mother, me, O Lord, standing in the need of pray'r.
Tempo I
39

43
me, it's me, O Lord, standing in the need of pray'r. It's
me, it's me, O Lord, standing in the need of pray'r. It's
me, it's me, O Lord, standing in the need of pray'r. It's
f
It's me, it's me, O Lord, standing in the need of pray'r.
f
It's me, it's me, O Lord, standing in the need of pray'r.
f
It's me, it's me, O Lord, standing in the need of it's me,
43
43
mp
me, it's me, O Lord, stand - ing in the need of pray'r. Not the
mf
mp
me, it's me, O Lord, stand - ing in the need of pray'r.
mp
me, it's me, O Lord, stand - ing in the need of pray'r.
mp
It's me, me, O Lord, stand - ing in the need of pray'r.
mp
It's me, me, O Lord, stand - ing in the need of pray'r.
mp
It's me, me, O Lord, stand - ing in the need of pray'r.
mp
mf
47

51
p
stran - ger nor the neigh - bour, but it's me, O Lord, standing in the need of pray'r. Not the
mf
nor the neigh - bour, but it's me, O Lord, stand-ing in the need of pray'r.
mf
neigh - bour, but it's me, O Lord, stand-ing in the need of pray'r.
mf
but it's me, O Lord, stand-ing in the need of pray'r.
mf
me, O Lord, stand-ing in the need of pray'r.
mf
and I'm stand-ing in the need of pray'r.
51
p
51

stran - ger nor the neigh- bour, but it's me, O Lord, and I'm stand-ing in the need of pray'r.
p
nor the neigh- bour, but it's me, O Lord, stand-ing in the need of pray'r.
p
neigh- bour, but it's me, O Lord, stand-ing in the need of pray'r. It's
p
but it's me, O Lord, stand-ing in the need of pray'r.
p
me, O Lord, stand-ing in the need of pray'r.
p
me, O Lord, It's me,
55

59
It's me, O Lord, standing in the need of pray'r.
It's me, me, O Lord, standing in the need of pray'r.
me, it's me, O Lord, standing in the need of pray'r. It's
me, O Lord, standing in the need of pray'r. It's
It's me,
pp
It's me, O Lord, standing in the need of pray'r. It's
It's me, me, O Lord, standing in the need of pray'r. It's
me, it's me, O Lord, and I'm standing in the need of pray'r. It's
me, it's me, O Lord, standing in the need of pray'r.
it's me, me, O Lord, It's me,
me, O Lord, It's me,
ff
63

67
me, it's me, O Lord, It's
me, it's me, O Lord, stand-ing in the need of pray'r. It's
me, it's me, O Lord, stand-ing in the need of pray'r. It's
It's me, me, O Lord, stand-ing in the need of pray'r.
it's me, me, O Lord, stand-ing in the need of pray'r.
it's me, me, O Lord, It's me,
67
71
rit.
ten.
me, it's me, O Lord, stand-ing in the need of pray'r.
me, it's me, O Lord, stand-ing in the need of pray'r.
me, it's me, O Lord, stand-ing in the need of pray'r.
It's me, me, O Lord, stand-ing in the need of pray'r.
It's me, me, O Lord, stand-ing in the need of pray'r.
it's me, me, O Lord, stand-ing in the need of pray'r.

Swing Low, Sweet Chariot

For SATTBB a cappella
Performance Time: Approx. 2:30

Traditional Spiritual
Arranged by PETER KNIGHT

* Optional Alto

Sop.
Alto
Oo
com - ing for to car - ry me home.
Ten. I
(mel.)
Oo
com - ing for to car - ry me home.
Ten. II
Oo
com - ing for to car - ry me home.
Bass I
Bass II
Swing low, sweet char - i - ot,
com - ing for to car - ry me home.
9
13
mp
Swing low, sweet char - i - ot, com - ing for to car - ry me
mp
Swing low, sweet char - i - ot, com - ing for to car - ry me
mp
Swing low, sweet char - i - ot, com - ing for to car - ry me
mp
Swing low, sweet char - i - ot, com - ing for to car - ry me
13
13

com - ing for to car - ry me home.
home. Swing low, sweet char - i - ot,
home. Swing low, sweet char - i - ot,
home. Swing low, sweet char - i - ot,
Unis.
home. Swing low, sweet char - i - ot,
16
21
poco rit.
a tempo
mp
com-ing for to car - ry me home. Oo
poco rit.
(mel.)
a tempo
mp
com-ing for to car - ry me home. Oo
poco rit.
a tempo
mp
com-ing for to car - ry me home. Oo
poco rit.
Unis.
mf a tempo
com-ing for to car - ry me home. I looked o - ver Jor - dan, what did I see,
21
poco rit.
a tempo
19

mf
mf
mf
f
coming for to carry me home? A band of angels
mf
23
p
coming,
p (mel.)
coming for to carry me home.
p
coming for to carry me home
p
coming after me, coming for to carry me home
p
26

29
f
char - i - ot,
Unis.
Swing low, sweet char - i - ot, com - ing for to car - ry me
Swing low, sweet char - i - ot, com - ing for to car - ry me
Swing low, sweet char - i - ot, com - ing for to car - ry me
Swing low, sweet char - i - ot, com - ing for to car - ry me
29
29
dim.
home. Swing low, sweet char - i - ot,
home. Swing low, sweet char - i - ot,
home. Swing low, sweet char - i - ot,
home. Swing low, sweet char - i - ot,
32

37
mp
p
Oo com - ing for to
mp
com - ing for to car - ry me home, com - ing for to
com - ing for to car - ry me home, com - ing for to
com - ing for to car - ry me home, com - ing for to
35
rit.
Unis.
car - ry me, Swing low, sweet char - i - ot, Swing low.
car - ry me home. Swing low.
car - ry me home. Swing low.
car - ry me home. Swing low.
38